THE
TOTALLY NINJA
RACCOONS
MEET THE
THUNDERBIRD

by Kevin Coolidge

Illustrated by Jubal Lee

The Totally Ninja Raccoons Are:

Rascal:
He's the shortest brother and loves doughnuts. He's great with his paws and makes really cool gadgets. He's a little goofy and loves both his brothers, even when they pick on him, but maybe not right then.

Bandit:
He's the oldest brother. He's tall and lean. He's super smart and loves to read. He leads the Totally Ninja Raccoons, but he couldn't do it by himself.

Kevin:
He may be the middle brother, but he refuses to be stuck in the middle. He has the moves and the street smarts that the Totally Ninja Raccoons are going to need, even if it does sometimes get them into trouble as well as out of trouble.

CONTENTS

"It's gone! It looks like it's been ripped out of the ground!"

1

SINK OR SWIM?

Moths flutter around the soft glow of the gaslights lining the Main Street of Wellsboro. It's a warm summer night, and the Totally Ninja Raccoons are walking to the Green.

Bandit confidently strolls along in the lead. Kevin twirls his staff like a baton, and Rascal trails behind.

Rascal is walking slower than usual. He's wearing a pink flamingo flotation device around his waist. It's causing him to walk with a waddle.

"Guys, wait up! I have short legs!" yells Rascal.

"Why are you wearing that?" asks Kevin.

"I can't swim," says Rascal.

Bandit stops, turns around, and puts his paws on his hips and looks at Kevin and Rascal.

"A Ninja Raccoon needs to have many skills. Among those should be stealth aaand swimming," says Bandit.

"But I don't know how to swim," says Rascal.

1

"Or how to be quiet," says Bandit.

"Bandit and I are going to teach you how to swim," says Kevin.

"And that's why I am wearing a flotation device, says Rascal.

Bandit reaches into his backpack and pulls out a book called *How to Swim in Ten Easy Lessons*.

"The first goal is to get you over the fear of water," says Bandit.

"I'm not afraid of water. I just prefer a cold birch beer," says Rascal.

"I mean your fear of drowning," says Bandit.

"That's why I'm wearing Pinkie," says Rascal.

"You might not always have 'Pinkie' to rely on," says Kevin.

"I did have my eye on Yellow Duckie, but I found this outside our clubhouse. I look great in it. I don't want to wear what everyone else is wearing," says Rascal.

"We'll take it slow. You need to feel safe. We'll start you out in the shallow end and let you splash around," says Bandit.

"Tonight we are going to swim in the fountain that surrounds the Wynken, Blynken and Nod statue. The water isn't very deep there," says Kevin.

"I can collect spare change and buy a birch beer from the soda machine by the grocery store. I love birch beer!" shouts Rascal.

"We know!" Kevin and Bandit say together.

"You aren't thinking of taking money from the fountain are you?" asks Bandit.

"Sure, it's just lying there waiting for someone to pick it up," replies Rascal.

"That money is for wishes, and it goes to charities to make those wishes come true," says Bandit.

"Taking it would be stealing those wishes," says Kevin.

"Let's focus on swimming. We need to get you used to the water first, and then you can take off that flotation device. It's going to give you poor body position," says Bandit.

"I'll teach you to tread water when you are ready. It's not that hard," says Kevin.

"I can't even swim, and you want me to walk on water?" says Rascal.

"No, silly, treading water is part of swimming that involves your staying upright within a body of water, and keeping your head above water," says Bandit.

"If you ever forget what to do, don't panic, and just tread water," says Kevin.

"Are we there yet?" asks Rascal.

"The fountain is in the middle of the town Green where the statue of Wynken, Blynken and Nod is located," says Bandit.

"What?" says Kevin.

"The three human children in a wooden shoe," says Bandit.

Bandit stops walking and points his paw over to the middle of the Green. A bright flash of light temporarily blinds all three raccoons.

"My eyes! What was that? Hey, where's the statue?" yells Rascal.

There's no statue in the middle of the park. Just a big, deep hole where the statue is supposed to be.

"It's gone! It looks like it's been ripped out of the ground!" shouts Bandit.

"I never did understand how those three kids fit in that shoe," says Kevin.

"Someone must have stolen the statue!" shouts Bandit.

"Who'd want to steal a statue?" questions Kevin.

"Gypsy!" shout all three Ninja Raccoons together.

"Does this mean I don't have to go swimming?" asks Rascal.

"We need to find the statue," says Bandit.

"I don't see how that's our problem," says Kevin.

"The statue is very important to the town. A lot of people visit the statue and take photos," says Bandit.

"And throw coins in and make wishes, and drop their popcorn," says Rascal.

"We totally need to find that statue," says Bandit."Is it popcorn with extra butter?" asks Kevin.

"We totally need to recover the statue. We can do this, raccoons, because we are..." says Bandit.

"Not going swimming tonight?" asks Rascal.

"Hungry for popcorn?" asks Kevin.

"We are ninjas, and this is what we do!" shouts Bandit.

Bandit goes running back to the super-secret clubhouse. Kevin shrugs his shoulders and scurries behind him. Rascal slowly starts waddling back.

"I didn't want to go swimming anyway. Besides, I had a snack before we left. I'm not supposed to go swimming for at least an hour," says Rascal.

"I have a plan that will stop those meddling Ninja Raccoons for good"

2

NODDING OFF

Earlier that day at a hidden location: It's a super, secret meeting of the Cat Board, the mysterious organization that plots to take over the entire world, except for Antarctica. Cats find it too cold, even with a parka.

A large Siamese cat is sitting at a large, round table. Her tail is twitching back and forth. She looks angry.

"Those Ninja Raccoons need to be stopped!" shouts the Siamese cat.

A fat, calico cat calmly looks at the large Siamese cat, "I have a plan that will stop those meddling Ninja Raccoons for good."

"You've promised that before!" yowls the Siamese.

"This plan is brilliant. It will work for sure. We steal the Wynken, Blynken and Nod statue from the

Green in Wellsboro, and we blame it on the Ninja Raccoons. The Borough Council will then do our dirty work for us," mews Gypsy.

A small, nearly hairless cat speaks up, "How do we get the statue out? It's way too heavy for us to move. How will we shift the blame to the Ninja Raccoons?"

"We'll take their photo at the scene of the crime," chuckles Gypsy.

A black and white cat, that looks like he is wearing a tuxedo, rubs his paw on his chin, "Hmmm, I'm sure I could blow it up. All I need is some dynamite," says Huck.

"We could melt down all the pieces and buy sardines!" says an all black cat named Finn.

"Noooo! Sardines make you fart, Finn!" meows Huck.

"No, no, no, the legendary thunderbird will steal it for us. Besides, I will use this fountain for my new water bowl and to wash my paws," says Gypsy.

"Is this thunderbird creature good to eat?" asks Finn.

"This majestic bird lives in the forest surrounding the Pennsylvania Grand Canyon, and is the size of a small airplane, with the strength of a bulldozer," says Gypsy.

The nearly hairless cat speaks up,"Are you sure this is a good idea?" says the Sphinx.

"Of course, this huge bird will steal the statue, and we'll blame it on the Ninja Raccoons, and animal control will catch them," says Gypsy.

"This plan better work, Gypsy. You can be replaced," says the large Siamese cat.

"You'll see. You'll see. Leave it all up to me," laughs Gypsy.

"You guys are going to want to see this"

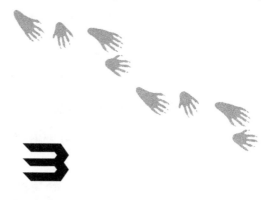

₃

FRAMED!

It's a hot, lazy afternoon at the secret clubhouse of the Ninja Raccoons. Bandit reads. Kevin snoozes, and Rascal tinkers with several spare parts.

Bandit picks up the newspaper. There, on the front page of the *Wellsboro Gazette*, is a photo of the Ninja Raccoons standing right next to the gaping hole where the Wynken, Blynken, and Nod statue used to be.

"You guys are going to want to see this," says Bandit.

Rascal perks up his ears and waddles over to see what Bandit is talking about. Kevin snorts and wakes up.

"Hey, that looks just like you, Bandit! And on the front page, too!" shouts Rascal.

"That's because it is me, and you, and Kevin. Of course, Kevin has his eyes shut. He never takes a good photo," says Bandit.

"Cool, your eyes are glowing red," says Rascal.

"It's just refraction of the light source," says Bandit.

Kevin opens one eye without moving and says," And why are we on the front page of the *Wellsboro Gazette*?"

"Masked Bandits Steal Famous Statue," reads Bandit.

"I know, right? I sure hope they catch those crooks," says Rascal.

"The paper is saying we are the thieves," says Bandit.

"It's not true! We're not thieves! We're ninjas!" shouts Rascal.

"I wouldn't worry. No one reads the *Wellsboro Gazette* anyway," says Kevin.

"We better hope not. The paper is calling for us to be punished. There's a reward for our capture and the editor of the paper says we should be sent to Animal Land as punishment for our crimes against humanity," says Bandit.

"I won't go back to Animal Land! I can't!" yells Rascal.

"Don't worry, Rascal. We're never going back, and no one reads his stupid editorials," says Kevin.

Kevin closes his eyes and tries to go back to sleep.

"Now we really need to recover the statue to clear our names," says Rascal.

"And to show we are ninjas!" exclaims Rascal.

"Can we do it later? I'm trying to sleep here," says Kevin.

"We'll need to examine the Green where the statue was stolen," says Bandit.

"We'll search for clues! My super-duper glasses can help," says Rascal.

"If I agree to help, will you guys let me go back to sleep?" asks Kevin.

"We'll recover the statue," says Bandit.

"And foil Gypsy's evil plan," says Rascal.

"We don't know for sure that Gypsy is behind this," says Bandit.

"Who else could it be? She's probably still mad, because we interrupted her naps," says Kevin.

"And stopped her plans to take over the world," says Rascal.

"If we are locked up in Animal Land, then she would take over the world. We are the only ninjas stopping her," says Bandit.

"We have to solve the mystery of the missing statue!" says Rascal.

"And then we'll take a nap?" asks Kevin.

"We can do this, because we are the totally...," shout Rascal and Bandit together.

"Tired raccoons?" questions Kevin.

"Let me have a closer look at that feather"

4

SCENE OF THE CRIME

Bandit, Rascal, and Kevin search for clues on the Green in Wellsboro.

"There's nothing here, guys, except the big hole where the statue was," says Kevin.

"There's always something. That's why we are here. To find a clue to clear our names," says Bandit.

Rascal wears his special glasses and is scouring the ground. He also wears his inflatable, pink flamingo.

"I still don't know how Gypsy knew we were going to be here last night," says Bandit.

"Rascal, why are you wearing Pinkie?" asks Kevin.

"I can't swim," answers Rascal.

"Have you found anything yet, Rascal?" asks Bandit.

Rascal spins around and points to a big, ugly bug that is on the back of the inflatable flamingo. The bug doesn't move.

"I found an insect on Pinkie," answers Rascal.

"Uggh, I hope it isn't another flyder," says Kevin.

"That's not a flyder, or an insect. It's a bug," says Bandit.

"That's what I said. It's a bug," says Rascal.

"It's a bug, an electronic listening device. That must be how Gypsy knew we were going to be here last night," says Bandit.

"Get it off! Get it off!" screams Rascal.

Kevin grabs a huge, black feather and flicks off the bug. It flies off and drops into the hole where the statue was.

"It's gone. That will really 'bug' Gypsy," says Kevin.

"Let me have a closer look at that feather, Kevin," says Bandit.

"It's huuuuge," says Rascal.

"It's the biggest feather I've ever seen. Even bigger than the emu feather at Animal Land," says Kevin.

"Exactly! I think we've found the thief," says Bandit.

Rascal looks around, "Where? I don't see an emu!"

"I believe this may be the feather of the legendary thunderbird, a creature of Native American myth," says Bandit.

"Well, the statue is mything..." says Rascal.

"Why would a bird steal a statue?" asks Kevin.

"Gypsy!" shout the Totally Ninja Raccoons.

"Well, according to the book, the thunderbird is an ancient bird of prey known as a teratorn. It eats meat."

5

BIRDS OF A FEATHER

The Ninja Raccoons gather around the table in their super-secret clubhouse hidden in a junkyard. Bandit opens a book with a picture of a huge, black bird, with a white-ringed neck, on the cover.

"According to this book, thunderbirds are real, and they have been spotted in parts of Tioga County," says Bandit.

"I thought you said they were a creature of myth, and not real?" says Kevin.

"The feather you found was over five feet long," says Bandit.

"Well, even if thunderbirds are real, how are we going to find a bird? Rascal can't swim, and none of us can fly," says Kevin.

"I'm working on both," says Rascal.

"We need to figure out a way to track this bird to its nest," says Bandit.

"Our friend Billy, the weird and wacky werewolf, could do it! He has a nose for trouble, and for General Tso's chicken," says Rascal.

"It has to be after school or on the weekend, though. Remember, he's a twelve year old boy in his human form," says Bandit.

"It's the full moon tonight. He's coming over to play ball and help me work the bugs out on my glove-launching system," says Rascal.

"Uggh, enough with the bugs already," complains Kevin.

"I'm going to revolutionize the way baseball is played. It's the future," says Rascal.

"Our future is the inside of a cage if we don't recover that statue," says Bandit.

"I'm **NOT** going back to Animal Land," says Kevin.

"Billy said he'd meet me in the junkyard after he finished his homework," says Rascal.

"The werewolf sure was a lot scarier before we found out his name was Billy," says Kevin.

"Who dares enter my domain?" booms the voice.

6

SEARCH FOR THE STATUE

The Totally Ninja Raccoons and Billy the werewolf hike in the woods near the Pennsylvania Grand Canyon. Rascal waves the five foot feather around.

"Are you sure the thunderbird is out here? This is the Pennsylvania Grand Canyon, and according to the book, they have never been spotted out here," says Bandit.

The weird and wacky werewolf opens his jaw, "Growl, woof, grrrrr,"

"Billy says the nose knows. The big bird is out here, and close," says Rascal.

"And just what are we going to do when we find this thunderbird?" says Kevin.

"We'll confirm the winged beast stole the statue, where the statue is hidden, and convince the big bird to return the statue and clear our names," states Bandit.

"Growl, grrr, wuff, wuff," says Billy the werewolf.

"Billy says it might not be quite so simple. A thunderbird does what it wants," says Rascal.

"We'll figure it out," says Kevin.

The Ninja Raccoons come upon a huge hemlock tree with a pile of bones and antlers under it. Billy the werewolf sniffs at a bone.

"Is that a skull?" asks Rascal.

"Ummm, just what does a thunderbird eat?" asks Kevin.

"Well, according to my readings, the thunderbird is most likely an ancient bird of prey known as a teratorn. It eats meat," says Bandit.

"Like General Tso's chicken?" asks Rascal.

"More like us!" says Kevin.

"According to the book, *Thunderbirds: Living Legends of Giant Birds*, they most likely ate carrion. That's the decaying flesh of dead animals," says Bandit.

"Ugggh! Stinky!" says Rascal.

A deep voice comes from above.

"Who dares enter my domain?" booms the voice.

"We're the Totally Ninja Raccoons!" shout the three Ninja Raccoons.

"Errf, wuff, growl, growl," growls Bill the werewolf.

"And Billy the werewolf," says Rascal.

"We're here to ask you to return the Wynken, Blynken and Nod statue," says Bandit.

"We need to prove our innocence and clear our names," says Rascal.

"I can't go back to Animal Land. I just can't," cries Kevin.

The giant bird is dark brown with a white ring around its neck. It looks like a turkey vulture, but much, much bigger. The thunderbird spreads its wings and looks down upon the Ninja Raccoons, and Billy the werewolf.

"It is not your concern what I do," says the thunderbird.

"It is! Gypsy the Cat, has blamed us for stealing the statue, and to clear our name we need to get the statue returned where it belongs," says Bandit.

"Hmmm, I'll return the statue if you can answer my riddle. Gypsy the Cat never kept her promise to me anyway. I owe her nothing! What is the creature that walks on four legs in the morning, two legs at noon, and three legs in the evening?" asks the thunderbird.

"That's easy! It's Billy the werewolf using Kevin's staff," says Rascal.

"Ummm, that's not the answer I was looking for," says the thunderbird.

"The answer you were looking for is a man. A human crawls on four legs when it is a baby. The 'morning' of your riddle," says Bandit.

"And on two legs in the middle of their life, or the 'noon' of your riddle," says Kevin.

"And in the evening of a man's life, a human will use a cane, or a really neat ninja staff as their third leg," says Rascal.

"Very good, Ninja Raccoons. I will return the statue," says the thunderbird.

"What promise did Gypsy make you?" asks Bandit.

"She promised she would teach me how to swim," says the thunderbird.

"That's silly. Cats don't swim," says Kevin.

"Tigers do!" says Bandit.

"It's OK, thunderbird. I can't swim either, but Kevin and Bandit are going to teach me!" says Rascal.

"Could you teach me to swim?" asks the thunderbird.

"Birds can't swim!" says Kevin.

"In fact, many birds can swim, and swimming is sort of like flying through water. I bet we could teach you the breast stroke," says Bandit.

"Oh, thank you! Thank you! I'll get that statue returned," says the thunderbird.

The three Ninja Raccoons climb onto the thunderbird and fly through the night-time sky, off to Gypsy's secret lair.

7

HAPPY RETURN

The Ninja Raccoons and Billy the werewolf stand around the tree looking at each other. Bandit looks at the thunderbird and asks, "How are you going to get the statue back?"

"I'm going to have to steal the statue back from Gypsy," says the thunderbird.

"That's really going to 'bug' her," says Rascal.

"Enough with the bug jokes already," says Kevin.

"How are you going to pull that off?" asks Bandit.

"She had me deliver it outside her secret lair. She's using it to soak her paws," says the thunderbird.

"Are you going to be able to get to it?" asks Bandit.

"She'll never see me coming. It's night. I might as well do it now," says the thunderbird.

"Grrr, wuff, wuff, growl," growls Billy, the werewolf.

29

"Billy says he has to head back to town before it's time to go to school," says Rascal.

"We should start the hike back to town," says Bandit.

"It's ten miles back to the clubhouse, and I have short legs...," says Rascal.

"I could give you a lift back to Wellsboro. I have to deliver the statue there anyway," says the thunderbird.

"We could fly back? Cool!" says Rascal.

"It'd save a considerable amount of time that I could spend reading instead," says Bandit.

"Or sleeping," says Kevin.

"We'll be just like Wynken, Blynken, and Nod, except we are three Ninja Raccoons, and we are riding a thunderbird instead of a wooden shoe," says Rascal.

"Yeah, we're cooler. I still don't see how those kids fit in a wooden shoe," says Kevin.

The three Ninja Raccoons climb onto the thunderbird and fly through the night-time sky, off to Gypsy's secret lair.

They fly through clouds and fog, and the thunderbird swoops down and picks up the statue with huge talons and flies towards the little town of Wellsboro.

"This would be great for gathering information for missions," says Bandit.

"I can see the Chinese restaurant from here!" shouts Rascal.

"I think I'm going to be sick," says Kevin.

The thunderbird soars over Wellsboro towards the Green. As he swoops down to drop off the statue, a man walking his dog early in the morning looks up in surprise.

The thunderbird sets the statue down and lands so the Ninja Raccoons can hop off.

"We didn't quite make the Green," says Bandit.

"Close enough. It's the Court House lawn. The Green is across the street. I could hit it with a baseball," says Kevin.

"Or with my glove-launching system," says Bandit.

"Our names will be cleared. Now let's get home before the sun rises," says Bandit.

"Yeah, I'm totally pooped," says Kevin.

Gypsy throws down the paper in disgust,
"Those darn Ninja Raccoons!"

8

GYPSY IS GRUMPY

Later that morning, Gypsy the cat grabs a doughnut and a copy of the newspaper.

"I'm going to soak my paws in my lovely new fountain, and read another in-depth editorial about how those pesky Ninja Raccoons should be caught and locked up in Animal Land," chuckles Gypsy.

Gypsy walks outside in the late morning sunshine, and loudly mews, "It's gone! My statue, my beautiful fountain is gone. It's, it's, it's stolen!" mewls Gypsy.

Gypsy throws down the paper in disgust, "Those darn Ninja Raccoons!" yowls Gypsy.

The paper lands face up with the headline showing.

MISSING STATUE MYSTERIOUSLY RETURNS. RACCOONS ARE INNOCENT!

THE END

About the Thunderbird

The thunderbird is a creature from Native American myth. It is considered a supernatural bird of great strength and power. The thunderbird's name comes from the belief that the beating of its enormous wings stirs the wind and causes thunder. It is powerful, intelligent and all agree you don't want to make the thunderbird angry.

Some people think thunderbirds could be real, and have claimed to have seen them. Reports go back hundreds of years, and scientists have proven that giant birds called teratorns once existed with wingspans between 12 and 18 feet. Big birds are nothing new to the woods of Tioga County. We have bald eagles in the canyon, as well as osprey, and turkey vultures.

Giant-bird reports continue, though some people would like to dismiss such sightings. It's true it can be hard to gauge distance and poor lighting can play tricks on eyes. A giant bird would leave a trace, or maybe - just maybe - Tioga County with its forests and swamps, offers a place where the thunderbird can linger and be seen by a lucky few.

Do you think giant birds are real? Does the thunderbird exist? Did it once fly the skies? Is there such a creature alive and in the woods today? Or is it just a story and legend? Read more, become a reading ninja, and decide for yourself.

About the Author

Kevin resides in Wellsboro, just a short hike from the Pennsylvania Grand Canyon. When he's not writing, you can find him at *From My Shelf Books & Gifts*, an independent bookstore he runs with his wife, several helpful employees, and two friendly cats, Huck & Finn.

He's recently become an honorary member of the Cat Board, and when he's not scooping the litter box, or feeding Gypsy her tuna, he's writing more stories about the Totally Ninja Raccoons. Be sure to catch their next big adventure, *The Totally Ninja Raccoons and the Catmas Caper.*

You can write him at:

From My Shelf Books & Gifts
7 East Ave., Suite 101
Wellsboro, PA 16901

www.wellsborobookstore.com

About the Illustrator

Jubal Lee is a former Wellsboro resident who now resides in sunny Florida, due to his extreme allergic reaction to cold weather.

He is an eclectic artist who, when not drawing raccoons, werewolves, and the like, enjoys writing, bicycling, and short walks on the beach.